FAT TALE

Eat Well & Exercise

Karen Land

By Karen Land

AuthorHouse™
1663 Liberty Drive, Suite 200
Bloomington, IN 47403
www.authorhouse.com
Phone: 1-800-839-8640

AuthorHouse™ UK Ltd.
500 Avebury Boulevard
Central Milton Keynes, MK9 2BE
www.authorhouse.co.uk
Phone: 08001974150

First published by AuthorHouse 3/29/2007

ISBN: 978-1-4259-7945-4 (sc)

Library of Congress Control Number: 2006910919

Printed in the United States of America
Bloomington, Indiana

This book is printed on acid-free paper.

Bloomington, IN Milton Keynes, UK

authorHOUSE®

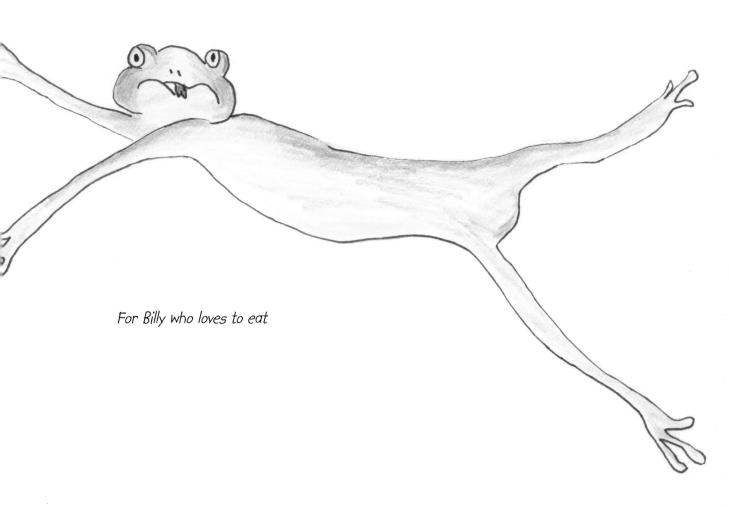

For Billy who loves to eat

Frogs

Frogs live in moist places, near ponds, streams and lakes.

They are carnivores. Frogs like to eat insects, worms and sometimes tiny fish.

Frogs' tongues zap out when a bug or fly flits by. Because their tongues are very sticky their prey is easily snared. Their tongues are unique. They are attached to the front of their mouths to make swallowing their prey easier.

Frogs enjoy the rain. They like to keep their skin moist and a rainy day makes hunting on land easier.

In the winter frogs bury themselves in mud or find a place to sleep quietly on the bottom of a lake, behind a sunken log or nestled under soggy leaves. Although we say they hibernate, scientists say frogs estivate. Their bodies have some natural antifreeze chemicals built in and they are able to slow down their body processes. A few kinds of frogs, who live in extremely cold climates, can survive even when frozen solid.

Frogs are amazing
AMPHIBIANS.

In the early morning, Froggie swooshed through the water to his favorite lily pad.

He zapped out his tongue and caught a disgusting gnat. Washing it down with a gulp of water, he groaned, "Grebit. That dinky gnat is not my idea of food. And I am a VERY hungry frog!" So Froggie stuck out his tongue and caught a water bug. The water bug took quite some time to swallow, but Froggie managed. "Yuck," he croaked. "I don't much care for water bugs either."

His whole family gathered around, busily chatting and eating.

"Froggie, try that dragonfly," said one of his cousins. "They're much tastier than water bugs."

Froggie took a bite. "You're right, they are better than water bugs," he added, but he twitched as he ate it up.

The next day, two kids came down to the tiny pond. They spied Froggie sitting on his lily pad, eating gnats and dragonflies. "Wow, will you look at that adorable little frog," said Shauna.

"He's the cutest frog I ever saw," said Willy.

"Yeah, but he seems to dislike eating dragonflies," said Shauna. "See him shudder when he zaps one with his tongue? Maybe he'll eat some of our fries."

"Throw him some," said Willy.

"Let's come back to the pond tomorrow with more fries for that crazy frog," said Willy.

"Yeah, and let's see if he likes Crispy Crunchies, too," said Shauna.

"You know," she added, "I think we should call him Gorf."

"Yup, he goes 'GORF' every time his lips smack around food."

The next day, Willy and Shauna sauntered down to the pond along with Jim, Shauna's big brother. "Jim, can you see him?" asked Willy, pointing with his chubby finger.

"Yep, I see him. He's the cutest little frog in the pond," said Jim.

"We call him Gorf because of the 'gorffie' sound he makes when he eats," said Shauna, making a GORF herself, as she crunched into a fistful of chips.

"What are you kids going to feed Gorf?" asked Jim.

"Well, I brought along my favorite chips and some awesome cereal. It's all the colors of the rainbow," said Shauna.

"And I couldn't finish my third burger yesterday, so I brought that, along with some candy bars," added Willy.

"That's not good food for frogs," said Jim. "And it's not good for you either!"

"We know, but Gorf loves french fries and so do we. Now we want to see if he loves some more of the same stuff we do," said Willy.

"Here, Gorf!" called Shauna. "Come and get it." She threw out a handful of sugar-coated multi-colored cereal. "This is what I had for breakfast. See if you like it too."

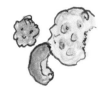

"I can't look," said Jim when he saw the froggie swimming toward them.

They laughed while Gorf gobbled up everything. GORF, GORF, GORRRFFF!

Then Willy threw the old leftover burger bits to Gorf. He gobbled them up too.

Gorf had a funny, stuffy feeling in his tummy.

Meanwhile, Shauna had finished off her chips and Willy was working on his second candy bar.

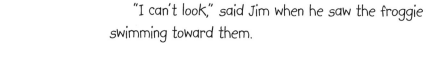

"It's not fair," said Jim. "Just because you two are always eating junk, you don't have the right to make that cute frog sick and overweight."

Willy and Shauna ignored Jim. They walked home in silence. Jim walked on ahead. Willy and Shauna dragged their feet. They were tired as usual.

"Let's see if Gorf likes pizza tomorrow," said Shauna.

"Whew, let's go and relax. Want to watch TV?" asked Willy.

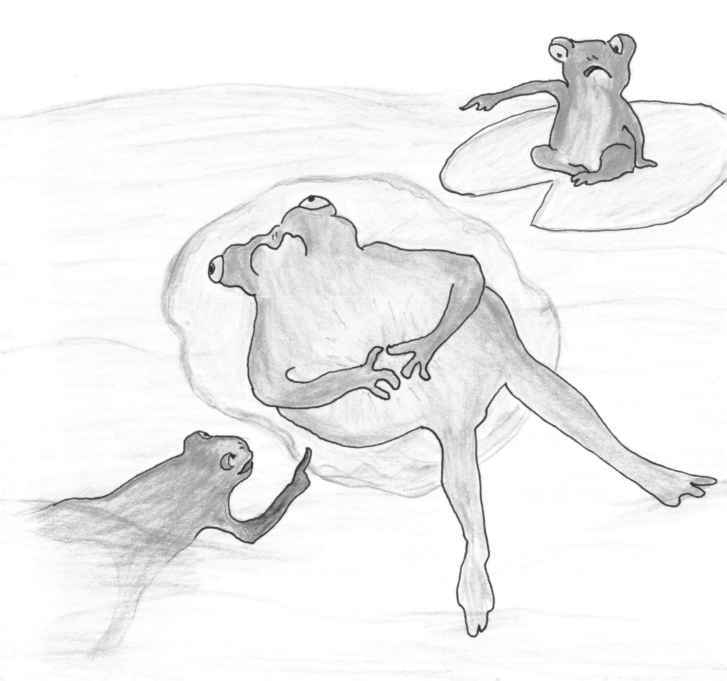

Poor, poor Gorf. His tummy hurt and his brothers, sisters, cousins, uncles, and aunts all scolded him for eating junk food. "How are you going to dive to the bottom of the pond to hibernate?" they asked. "Fat floats! If you can't dive to the bottom, you will freeze to death!"

"But that food tastes great," argued Gorf.

With great difficulty, Gorf climbed onto his favorite lily pad. The lily pad sank a tad below the water. "Oh," thought Gorf, "I am getting big."

"Oooh, and my tummy still hurts," he said, belching.

During the following weeks, Shauna and Willy spent many afternoons

down at the pond, feeding the frog and feeding themselves. They gave Gorf cookies and bagels, donuts and cake. Gorf ate it all, and so did they.

One day, Shauna said, "Gorf can't fit on his lily pad anymore."

Willy said, "I can't fit in any of my shorts anymore."

"Me either," said Shauna.

"Look at Gorf. He is so fat, he can't even swim," said Willy.

"And I noticed that he can't dive and swim underwater anymore," added Shauna.

Willy and Shauna looked at each other. They looked at Gorf. Jim was right. "We've all got to stop," they said together. All three looked very sad.

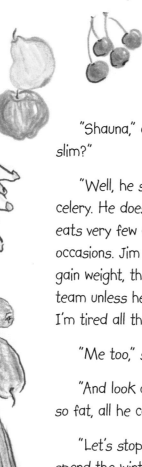

"Shauna," asked Willy, "how does Jim stay so slim?"

"Well, he snacks on apples, pears, carrots, and celery. He doesn't eat a lot of chips or fries. He eats very few cookies, or a slice of cake on special occasions. Jim loves soccer, and when he started to gain weight, the coach said he wouldn't make the team unless he could run fast without getting tired. I'm tired all the time," said Shauna.

"Me too," said Willy.

"And look at that poor frog," said Shauna. "He's so fat, all he can do is float."

"Let's stop feeding Gorf," said Willy. "So he can spend the winter with his family in the mud at the bottom of the pond."

Gorf blinked his eyes as if he understood.

"And let's get Jimmy to help us lose weight," said Shauna.

With that, the two kids put their snack food in the garbage container. They turned and headed home to find Jim.

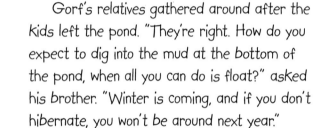

Gorf's relatives gathered around after the kids left the pond. "They're right. How do you expect to dig into the mud at the bottom of the pond, when all you can do is float?" asked his brother. "Winter is coming, and if you don't hibernate, you won't be around next year."

"I've got to change my eating habits," said Gorf. "Gnats, water bugs, and dragonflies from now on."

"Right on," said all his relatives.

Meanwhile, Jim helped Shauna and Willy make a simple diet plan.

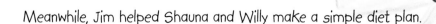